Anook
The Snow Princess

by Hans Wilhelm

BARRON'S

Far, far north, where
the polar winds blow,
is a land of ice and
snow called Northland.

In a huge palace lived a
mighty Polar Bear King
and his three daughters
– Aki, Taki and Anook.

Anook was the youngest and, of course,
the smallest Polar Bear Princess.
Her sisters teased her all the time.

Anook wished she could speak up,
but she was shy, and never knew
what to say. So she just kept quiet.

"Ladies!" said Tuk-tuk the royal seagull.
"You will never become queens if you
are so mean and cruel to Anook."

"Nonsense! I will be queen," insisted Aki.

"Oh no you won't. I will," growled Taki.

"Our father is very wise," whispered Anook.
"I am sure he'll choose the right one of us to
be the next queen."

One morning, Tuk-tuk gathered everyone
to listen to a royal announcement.

"Tonight," he squawked, "the king will
choose our next queen. He will choose
the daughter who shows him the most
love and loyalty."

"I'll write Father a wonderful poem," boasted Aki.

"I'll sing him a beautiful song," Taki said.

"Oh dear," thought Anook. "I'm too shy
to talk in front of everybody. Maybe
I could catch him a fish instead."

But Anook had never caught a
fish before. She tried all day long
without any luck.

She was about to give up, when
suddenly there was a loud splash.
Anook plunged her paw into the icy
water and caught a huge golden fish.
It wiggled and waggled, but she didn't
let go.

Proudly Anook carried the fish back
to the palace. She was so pleased
with her gift that she forgot to
watch where she was going and...

... CRASH!

Anook fell into a deep, dark hole
in the ice. The sides of the hole
were so steep and slippery that
she couldn't climb out again.

Finally, she heard voices above her.
"Please help me!" wailed Anook.

"Look who's here," said Aki. "Our
darling sister. Of course we will help
you. First, pass us your beautiful fish,
then we will pull you out."

Anook did exactly what they told her.
But as soon as her sisters had the fish,
they ran away, leaving Anook behind.

If Tuk-tuk hadn't heard her calling,
Anook would have frozen in the icy hole.

With the help of some royal foxes,
Tuk-tuk pulled Anook out.

"Quick, Anook. Hurry back to the palace,"
said Tuk-tuk. "The king is waiting for you."

Back at the palace, Aki was reading her poem,
   "I love you more than lollipops
   Or green sardines with honey drops.
   I love you, Dad, with all my heart,
   Because you are so big and smart."

Next it was Taki's turn. She sang her song,
   "Daddy Bear, oh Daddy Bear,
   I love you the most, I truly swear.
   Your coat's so white and very long.
   Your arms are big and super strong."

The king smiled with delight.

"Father," said Aki, "to show you
how much we love you, we caught
this beautiful golden fish for you."

"Now, Anook, it's your turn," said the king.
"What do you want to say to me?"

Slowly Anook stepped forward. She was
so nervous that her throat was dry.
"I... I... I love you, Father," she whispered.

"Is that all?" roared the king. "Nothing more? Anook, you have displeased me greatly. Your sisters will both become queens of Northland, but I never want to see you again. Leave my palace, now!"

With tears in her eyes Anook fled
from the palace. She ran across
snow-covered fields, frozen seas
and icy mountains.

When she had no more strength
to run, and no more tears to cry,
Anook lay down to sleep.

Suddenly, she heard a little sob.
There, shivering in the snow,
was a tiny wolf cub.

"Hello, little one," said Anook gently.
"Are you lost too? Snuggle up
with me. I'll keep you warm."

Soon they were both fast asleep.

Next morning, when Anook and the cub woke up, two wolves were standing beside them.

"How can we ever thank you for saving our cub's life?" the wolves asked.

Shyly, Anook told them all about Northland and how her father had sent her away. Just as she was finishing her story, Anook turned around...

... GULP!

She couldn't believe it. One hundred pairs of eyes were watching her, one hundred pairs of ears were listening to her story.

"Stay with us, Anook," begged all the wolves. "Stay with us for as long as you like."

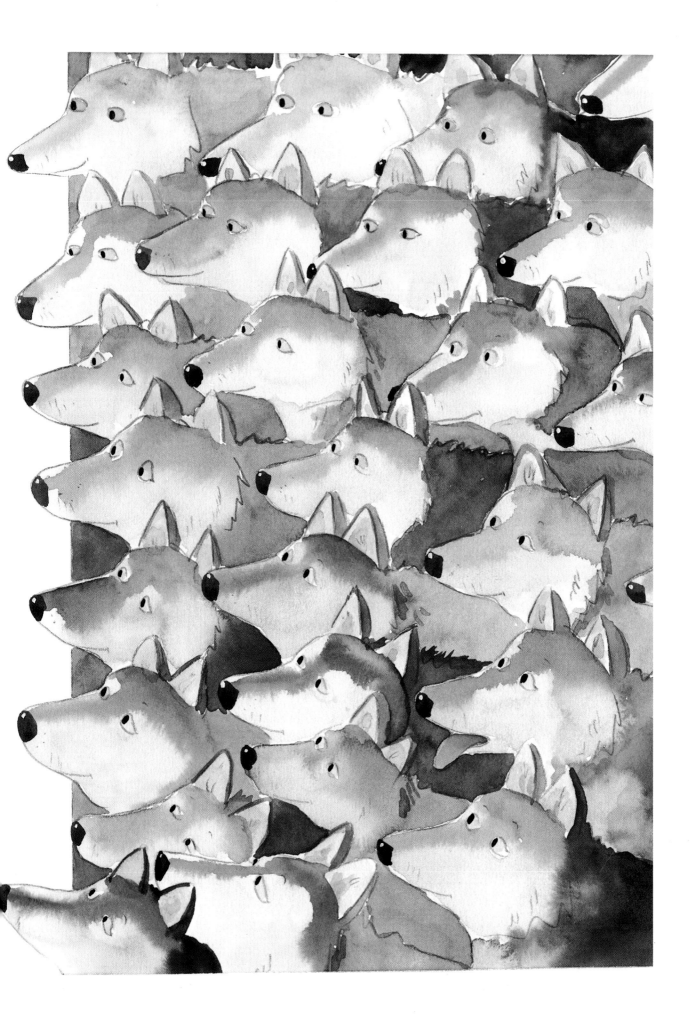

So Anook stayed with the wolves.
They taught her how to run and hunt,
and how to play. Every day, Anook and
the wolf cub grew bigger and stronger.
And so did their friendship.

One winter, Anook spotted a scrawny
gull resting on a rock.

"Tuk-tuk, is it you?" she asked.

"Anook!" cried the gull. "I am so
happy to see you. I've been
searching for you. Your father
needs you. When your sisters
became queens, they threw him
out of the palace."

"Quick, take me to my father,"
begged Anook.

They found the Polar Bear King in
a dark cave. He had grown so old
and weak that he could hardly stand up.
But when he saw Anook, tears ran down
his face and he hugged her tightly.

"Dear Anook," he cried. "Your sisters
have ruined Northland, and I treated you
cruelly and sent you away. Can you ever
forgive your silly old father?"

"Oh, Daddy," said Anook. "I love you.
My friends and I will take you home."

So Anook, her father, and all the wolves
set off for Northland, and the royal palace.

When they reached the palace gates,
the guards were happy to let them in.
They remembered how kind the king
and Anook had been.

When Aki and Taki saw Anook, they screamed,
"Get out! This is our palace."

But Anook was no longer afraid of her
sisters. Growing up with the wolves had made
her brave and strong. She gave such a loud roar,
that Aki and Taki turned and ran away as fast as
they could. Luckily, they were never seen again.

"Northland is free again. Anook has saved us!" everyone shouted.

"Don't praise me," said Anook. "I'm just happy that my father is king again."

"No, Anook!" interrupted the king. "You must be queen now. You have shown us all how good and wise you have become. You will be a wonderful queen."

A cheer went through
the crowd,
"Hail, Queen Anook!"

And, of course, Anook was a good and wise queen,
who brought peace and happiness to Northland.